THE NEW UTOPIA

JEROME K. JEROME

Copyright © 2015 Jerome K. Jerome

All rights reserved.

ISBN: 1515252604
ISBN-13: 978-1515252603

THE NEW UTOPIA

I had spent an extremely interesting evening. I had dined with some very "advanced" friends of mine at the "National Socialist Club". We had had an excellent dinner: the pheasant, stuffed with truffles, was a poem; and when I say that the '49 Chateau Lafitte was worth the price we had to pay for it, I do not see what more I can add in its favour.

After dinner, and over the cigars (I must say they do know how to stock good cigars at the National Socialist Club), we had a very instructive discussion about the coming equality of man and the nationalisation of capital.

I was not able to take much part in the argument myself, be- cause, having been left when a boy in a position which rendered it necessary for me to earn my own living, I have never enjoyed the time and opportunity to study these questions.

But I listened very attentively while my friends explained how, for the thousands of centuries during which it had existed before they came, the world had been going on all wrong, and how, in the course of the next few years or so, they meant to put it right.

Equality of all mankind was their watchword--perfect equality in all things--equality in possessions, and equality in position and influence, and equality in duties, resulting in equality in happiness and contentment.

The world belonged to all alike, and must be equally divided. Each man's labour was the property, not of himself, but of the State which fed and clothed him, and must be applied, not to his own aggrandisement, but to the enrichment of the race.

Individual wealth--the social chain with which the few had bound the many, the bandit's pistol by which a small gang of rob- bers had thieved--must be taken from the hands that too long had held it.

Social distinctions--the barriers by which the rising tide of humanity had hitherto been fretted and restrained--must be for ever swept aside. The human race must press onward to its destiny (whatever that might be), not as at present, a scattered horde, scrambling, each man for himself, over the broken ground of un- equal birth and fortune--the soft sward reserved for the feet of the pampered, the cruel stones reserved for the feet of the cursed,--but an ordered army, marching side by side over the level plain of equity and equality.

The great bosom of our Mother Earth should nourish all her children, like and like; none should be hungry, none should have too much. The strong man should not grasp more than the weak; the clever should not scheme to seize more than the simple. The earth was man's, and the fulness thereof; and among all mankind it should be portioned out in even shares. All men were equal by the laws of man.

With inequality comes misery, crime, sin, selfishness, arrogance, hypocrisy. In a world in which all men were equal, there would exist no temptation to evil, and our natural nobility would assert itself.

When all men were equal, the world would be Heaven--freed from the degrading despotism of God.

We raised our glasses and drank to EQUALITY, sacred EQUALITY; and then ordered the waiter to bring us Green Char- treuse and more cigars.

I went home very thoughtful. I did not go to sleep for a long while; I lay awake; thinking over this vision of a new world that had been presented to me.

How delightful life would be, if only the scheme of my socialis- tic friends could be carried out. There would ne no more of this struggling and striving against each other, no more jealousy, no more disappointment, no more fear of poverty! The State would take charge of us from the hour we were born until we died, and provide for all our wants from the cradle to the coffin, both inclu- sive, and we should need to give no thought even to the matter. There would be no more hard work (three hours' labour a day would be the limit, according to our calculations, that the State would require from each adult citizen, and nobody would be allowed to do more--*I* should not be allowed to do more)--no poor to pity, no rich to envy--no one to look down upon us, no one for us to look down upon (not quite so pleasant this latter reflection)--all our life ordered and arranged for us--nothing to think about except the glorious destiny (whatever that might be) of

Humanity.

Then thought crept away to sport in chaos, and I slept.

***

When I awoke, I found myself lying under a glass case, in a high, cheerless room. There was a label over my head; I turned and read it. It ran as follows.

THIS MAN WAS FOUND ASLEEP IN A HOUSE IN LONDON, AFTER THE GREAT SOCIAL REVOLUTION OF 1899. FROM THE ACCOUNT GIVEN BY THE LANDLADY OF THE HOUSE, IT WOULD APPEAR THAT HE HAD ALREADY, WHEN DISCOVERED, BEEN ASLEEP FOR OVER TEN YEARS (SHE HAVING FORGOTTEN TO CALL HIM). IT W AS DECIDED, FOR SCIENTIFIC PURPOSES, NOT TO AWAKE HIM, BUT JUST TO SEE HOW LONG HE WOULD SLEEP ON, AND HE WAS ACCORDINGLY BROUGHT AND DEPOSITED IN THE 'MUSEUM OF CURIOSITIES', ON FEBRUARY 11TH, 1900.

Visitors are requested not to squirt water through the air-holes.

An intelligent-looking old gentleman, who had been arranging some stuffed lizards in an adjoining case, came over and took the cover off me.

"What's the matter?" he asked; "anything disturbed you?"

"No," I said; "I always wake up like this, when I feel I've had enough sleep. What century is this?"

"This," he said, "is the twenty-ninth century. You have been asleep for just one thousand years."

"Ah! well, I feel all the better for it," I replied, getting down off the table. "There's nothing like having one's sleep out."

"I take it you are going to do the usual thing." said the old gentleman to me, as I proceeded to put on my

clothes, which had been lying beside me in the case. "You'll want me to walk round the city with you, and explain all the changes to you, while you ask questions and make silly remarks?"

"Yes," I replied, "I suppose that's what I ought to do."

"I suppose so," he muttered. "Come on, and let's get it over," and he led the way from the room.

As we went downstairs, I said: "Well, is it all right, now?" "Is what all right?" he replied.

"Why, the world," I replied. "A few friends of mine were arranging, just before I went to bed, to take it to pieces and fix it up again properly. Have they got it all right by this time? Is everybody equal now, and sin and sorrow and all that sort of thing done away with?"

"Oh, yes," replied my guide; "you'll find everything all right now. We've been working away pretty hard at things while you've been asleep. We've just got this earth about perfect now, I should say. Nobody is allowed to do anything wrong or silly; and as for equality, tadpoles ain't in it with us."

(He talked in rather a vulgar manner, I thought; but I did not like to reprove him.)

We walked out into the city. It was every clean and very quiet. The streets, which were designated by numbers, ran out from each other at right angles, and all presented exactly the same appearance. There were no horses or carriages about; all the traffic was conducted by electric cars. All the people that we met wore a quiet grave expression, and were so much like each other as to give one the idea that they were all members of the same family. Everyone was dressed, as was also my guide, in a pair of grey trousers, and a grey tunic, buttoning tight round the neck and fastened round the waist by a belt. Each man was clean shaven, and each man had black hair.

I said.

"Are all men twins?"

"Twins! Good gracious, no!" answered my guide. "Whatever made you fancy that?"

"Why, they all look so much alike," I replied; "and they've all got black hair!"

"Oh; that's the regulation colour for hair," explained my companion: "we've all got black hair. If a man's hair is not black naturally, he has to have it dyed black."

"Why?" I asked.

"Why!" retorted the old gentleman, somewhat irritably. "Why, I thought you understood that all men were now equal. What would become of our equality if one man or woman were allowed to swagger about in golden hair, while another had to put up with carrots? Men have not only got to be equal in these happy days, but to look it, as far as can be. By causing all men to be clean shaven, and all men and women to have black hair cut the same length, we obviate, to a certain extent, the errors of Nature."

I said.

"Why black?"

He said he did not know, but that was the colour which had been decided upon.

"Who by?" I asked.

"By THE MAJORITY," he replied, raising his hat and lowering his eyes, as if in prayer.

We walked further, and passed more men. I said.

"Are there no women in this city?"

"Women!" exclaimed my guide. "Of course there are. We've passed hundreds of them!"

"I thought I knew a woman when I saw one," I observed; "but I can't remember noticing any."

"Why, there go two, now," he said, drawing my attention to a couple of persons near to us, both dressed in the regulation grey trousers and tunics.

"How do you know they are women?" I asked.

"Why, you see the metal numbers tha everybody wears on their collar?"

"Yes: I was just thinking what a number of policeman you had, and wondering where the other people were!"

"Well, the even numbers are women; the odd numbers are men."

"How very simple," I remarked. "I suppose after a little practice you can tell one sex from the other almost at a glance?"

"Oh yes," he replied, "if you want to." We walked on in silence for a while. And then I said: "Why does everybody have a number?"

"To distinguish him by," answered my companion. "Don't people have names, then?" "No." "Why?"

"Oh! There was so much inequality in names. Some people were called Montmorency, and they looked down on the Smiths; and the Smythes did not like mixing with the Joneses: so, to save further bother, it was decided to abolish names altogether, and to give everybody a number."

"Did the Montmorencys and the Smythes object."

"Yes: but the Smiths and Joneses were in THE MAJORITY."

"And did no the Ones and Twos look down upon the Threes and Fours, and so on?"

"At first, yes. But, with the abolition of wealth, numbers lost their value, except for industrial purposes and for double acrostics, and now No. 100 does not consider himself in any way superior to No. 1,000,000."

I had not washed when I got up, there being no conveniences for doing so in the Museum, and I was beginning to feel somewhat hot and dirty. I said.

"Can I wash myself anywhere?"

He said.

"No; we are not allowed to wash ourselves. You must wait until half-past four, and then you will be washed for tea."

"Be washed!" I cried. "Who by?"

"The State."

He said that they had found they could not maintain their equality when people were allowed to wash themselves. Some people washed three or four times a day, while others never touched soap and water from one year's end to the other, and in consquence there got to be two distinct classes, the Clean and the Dirty. All the old class prejudices began to be revived. The clean despised the dirty, and the dirty hated the clean. So, to end dissension, the State decided to do the washing itself, and each citizen was now washed twice a day by government-appointed officials; and private washing was prohibited.

I noticed that we passed no houses as we went along, only block after block of huge, barrack-like buildings, all of the same size and shape. Occasionally, at a corner, we came across a smaller building, labelled "Museum", "Hospital", "Debating Hall", "Bath", "Gymnasium", "Acadeny of Sciences", "Exhibition of Industries", "School of Talk", etc., etc.; but never a house.

I said.

"Doesn't anybody live in this town?"

He said.

"You do ask silly questions; upon my word, you do. Where do you think they live?"

I said.

"That's just what I've been trying to think. I don't see any houses anywhere!"

He said.

"We don't need houses--not houses such as you are thinking of. We are socialistic now; we live together in

fraternity and equality. We live in these blocks that you see. Each block accommodates one thousand citizens.

It contains one thousand beds--one hundred in each room--and bath-rooms and dressing-rooms in proportion, a dining-hall and kitchens. At seven o'clock every morning a bell is rung, and ever one rises and tidies up his bed. At seven-thirty they go into the dressing-rooms, and are washed and shaved and have their hair done. At eight o'clock breakfast is served in the dining-hall. It comprises a pint of oatmeal porridge and half-a-pint of warm milk for each adult citizen. We are all strict vegetarians now. The vegetarian vote increased enormously during the last century, and their organisation being very perfect, they have been able to dictate every election for the past fifty years. At one o'clock another bell is rung, and the people return to dinner, which consists of beans and stewed fruits, with rolly-polly pudding twice a week, and plum-duff on Saturdays. At five o'clock there is tea, and at ten the lights are put out and everbody goes to bed. We are all equal, and we all live alike--clerk and scavenger, tinker and apothecary--all together in fraternity and liberty. The men live in blocks on this side of town, and the women are at the other end of the city."

"Where are the married people kept?" I asked.

"Oh, there are no married couples," he replied; "we abolished marriage two hundred years ago. You see, married life did not work at all well with our system. Domestic life, we found, was thoroughly anti-socialistic in its tendencies. Men thought more of their wives and families than they did of the State. They wished to labour for the benefit of their little circle of beloved ones rather than for the good of the community. They cared more for the future of their children than for the Destiny of Humanity. The ties of love and blood bound men together fast in little groups instead of in one great whole. Before considering the advancement of the human race, men considered the advancement of their kith and kin. Before striving for the greatest happiness of the greatest number, men strove for the happiness of the few who were near and dear to them. In secret, men and women hoarded up and laboured and denied themselves, so as, in secret, to give some little extra gift of joy to their beloved. Love stirred the vice of ambition in men's hearts. To win the smiles of the women they loved, to leave a name behind them that their children might be proud to bear, men sought to raise themselves above the general level, to do some deed that should make the world look up to them and honour them above their fellow-men, to press a deeper footprint than another's upon the dusty high-way of the age. The fundamental principles of Socialism were being daily thwarte and contemned. Each house was a revolutionary centre for the propagation of individualism and personality. From the warmth of each domestic hearth grew up the vipers, Comradeship and Independence, to sting the State and poison the minds of men.

"The doctrines of equality were openly disputed. Men, when they loved a woman, thought her superior to every other woman, and hardly took any pains to disguise their opinion. Loving wives believed their husbands to be wiser and braver and better than all other men. Mothers laughed at the idea of their children being in no way superior to other children. Children imbibed the hideous heresy that their father and mother were the best father and mother in the world.

"From whatever point you looked at it, the Family stood forth as our foe. One man had a charming wife and two sweet-tempered children; his neighbour was married to a shrew, and was the father of eleven noisy, ill-dispositioned brats--where was the equality.

"Again, wherever the Family existed, there hovered, ever contending, the angels of Joy and Sorrow; and in a world where joy and sorrow are known, Equality cannot live. One man and woman, in the night, stand weeping beside a little cot. On the other side of the lath-and-plaster, a fair young couple, hand in hand, are laughing at the silly antics of a grace-faced, gurgling baby. What is poor Equality doing.

"Such things could not be allowed. Love, we saw, was our enemy at every turn. He made equality impossible.

He brought joy and pain, and peace and suffering in his train. He disturbed men's beliefs, and imperilled the Destiny of Humanity; so we abolished him and all his works.

"Now there are no marriages, and, therefore, no domestic troubles; no wooing, therefore, no heartaching; no loving, therefore no sorrowing; no kisses and no tears.

"We all live together in equality free from the troubling of joy and pain."

I said.

"It must be very peaceful; but, tell me--I ask the question merely from a scientific standpoint--how do you keep up the supply of men and women?"

He said:

"Oh, that's simple enough. How did you, in your day, keep up the supply of horses and cows? In the spring, so many children, according as the State requires, are arranged for, and carefully bred, under medical supervision. When they are born, they are taken away from their mothers (who, else, might grow to love them), and brought up in the public nurseries and schools until they are fourteen. They are then examined by State-appointed inspectors, who decide what calling they shall be brought up to, and to such calling they are thereupon apprenticed. At twenty they take their rank of citizens, and are entitled to a vote. No difference whatever is made between men and women. Both sexes enjoy equal privileges."

I said.

"What are the privileges?"

He said.

"Why, all that I've been telling you."

We wandered on for a few more miles, but passed nothing but street after street of these huge blocks. I said.

"Are there no shops nor stores in this town?"

"No," he replied. "What do we want with shops and stores? The State feeds us, clothes us, houses us, doctors us, washes and dresses us, cuts our corns, and buries us. What could we do with shops?"

I began to feel tired with our walk. I said.

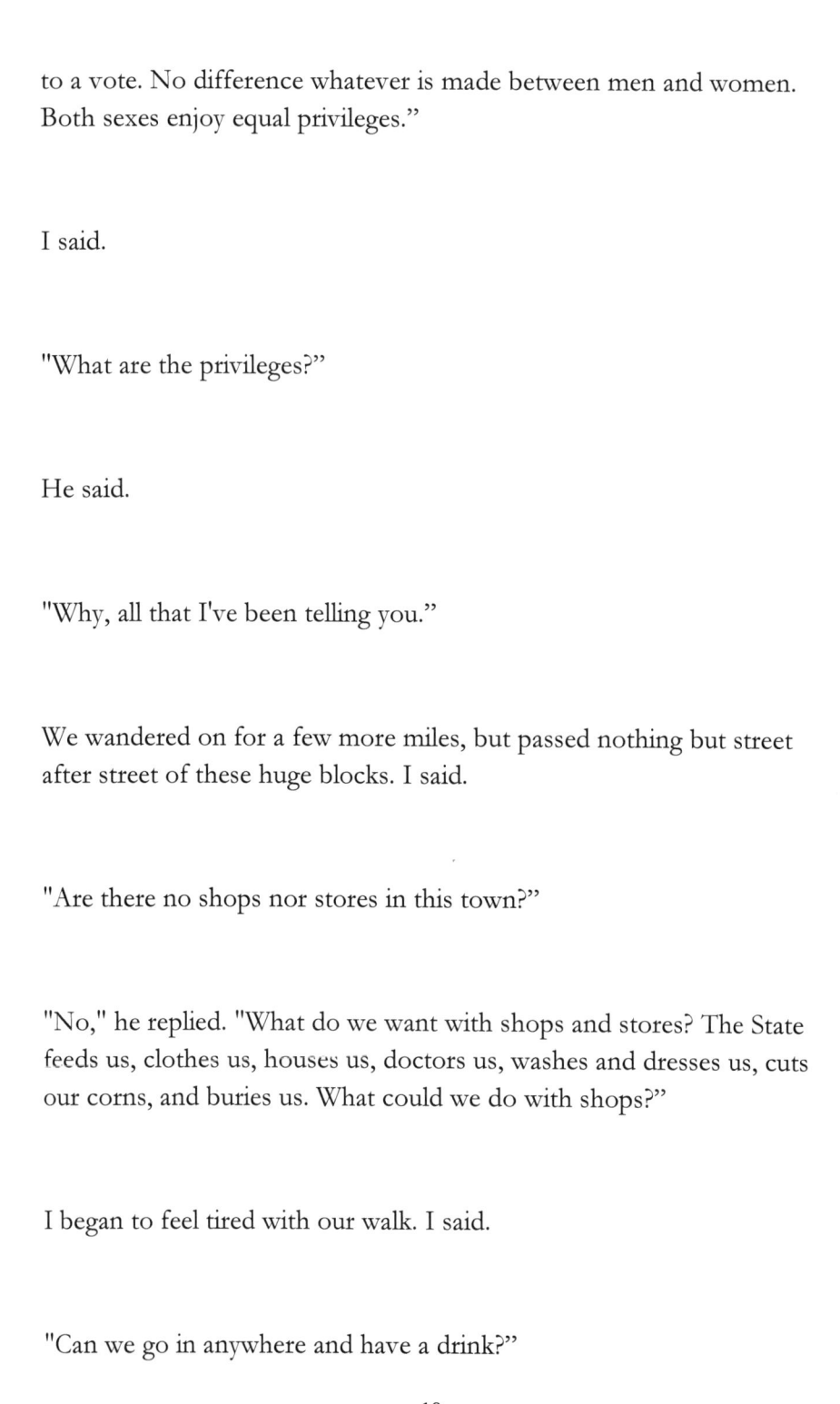

"Can we go in anywhere and have a drink?"

He said: "A 'drink'! What's a 'drink'? We have half-a-pint of cocoa with our dinner. Do you mean that?"

I did not feel equal to explaining the matter to him, and he evidently would not have understood me if I had; so I said.

"Yes; I meant that."

We passed a very fine-looking man a little further on, and I noticed that he had one arm. I had noticed two or three rather big-looking men with only one arm in the course of the morning, and it struck me as curious. I remarked about it to my guide.

He said.

"Yes; when a man is much above the average size and strength, we cut one of his legs or arms off, so as to make things more equal; we lop him down a bit, as it were. Nature, you see, is somewhat behind the times; but we do what we can to put her straight."

I said.

"I suppose you can't abolish her?"

"Well not altogether," he replied. "We only wish we could. But," he added afterwards, with pardonable pride, "we've done a good deal."

I said.

"How about an exceptionally clever man. What do you do with him?"

"Well, we are not much troubled in that way now," he answered. "We have not come across anything dangerous in the shape of brain-power for some considerable time now. When we do, we perform a surgical operation upon the head, which softens the brain down to the average level.

"I have sometimes thought," mused the old gentleman, "that it was a pity we could not level up sometimes, instead of always levelling down; but, of course, that is impossible."

I said.

"Do you think it right of you to cut these people up, and tone them down, in this manner?"

He said.

"Of course, it is right."

"You seem very cock-sure about the matter," I retorted. "Why is it 'of course' right?"

"Because it was done by THE MAJORITY."

"How does that make it right?" I asked.

"A MAJORITY can do no wrong," he answered.

"Oh! is that what the people who are lopped off think?"

"They!" he replied, evidently astonished at the question. "Oh, they are in the minority, you know."

"Yes; but even the minority has a right to its arms and legs and heads, hasn't it?"

"A minority has NO rights," he answered.

I said.

"It's just as well to belong to the Majority, if you're thinking of living here, isn't it?"

He said.

"Yes; most of our people do. They seem to think it more convenient."

I was finding the town somewhat uninteresting, and I asked if we could not go into the country for a change.

My guide said.

"Oh, yes, certainly;" but did not think I should care much for it.

"Oh! but it used to be so beautiful in the country," I urged, "before I went to bed. There were great green trees,

and grassy, wind-waved meadows, and little rose-decked cottages, and - -"

"Oh, we've changed all that," interrupted the old gentleman; "it is all one huge market-garden now, divided by roads and canals cut at right angles to each other. There is no beauty in the country now whatever. We have abolished beauty; it interfered with our equality. It was not fair that some people should live among lovely scenery, and other upon barren moors. So we have made it all pretty much alike everywhere now, and no place can lord it over another."

"Can a man emigrate into any other country?" I asked; "it doesn't matter what country--any other country would do."

"Oh, yes, if he likes," replies my companion; "but why should he? All lands are exactly the same. The whole world is all one people now--one language, one law, one life."

"Is there no variety, no change anywhere," I asked. "What do you do for pleasure, for recreation? Are there any theatres?"

"No," responded my guide. "We had to abolish theatres. The histrionic temperament seemd utterly unable to accept the principles of equality. Each actor thought himself the best actor in the world, and superior, in fact, to most other people altogether, I don't know whether it was the same in your day?"

"Exactly the same," I answered, "but we did not take any notice of it."

"Ah! we did," he replied, "and, in consequence, shut the theatres up. Besides, our White Ribbon Vigilance Society said that all places of amusement were vicious and degrading; and being an energetic and stout-winded band, they soon won THE MAJORITY over to their views; and so all amusements are prohibited now."

I said: "Are you allowed to read books?"

"Well," he answered, "there are not many written. You see, owing to our all living such perfect lives, and there being no wrong, or sorrow, or joy, or hope, or love, or grief in the world, and everything being so regular and proper, there is really nothing much to write about--except, of course, the Destiny of Humanity."

"True!" I said, "I see that. But what of the old works, the classics? You had Shakespeare, and Scott, and Thackeray, and there were one or two little things of my own that were not half-bad. What have you done with all those?"

"Oh, we have burned all those old works," he said. "They were full of the old, wrong notions of the old wrong, wicked times, when men were merely slaves and beasts of burden."

He said all the old paintings and sculptures had been likewise destroyed, partly for the same reason, and partly because they were considered improper by the White Ribbon Vigilance Society, which was a great power now; while all new art and literature were forbidden, as such things tended to undermine the principles of equality. They made men think, and the men that thought grew cleverer than those that did not want to think; and those that did not want to think naturally objected to this, and being in THE MAJORITY, objected to some purpose.

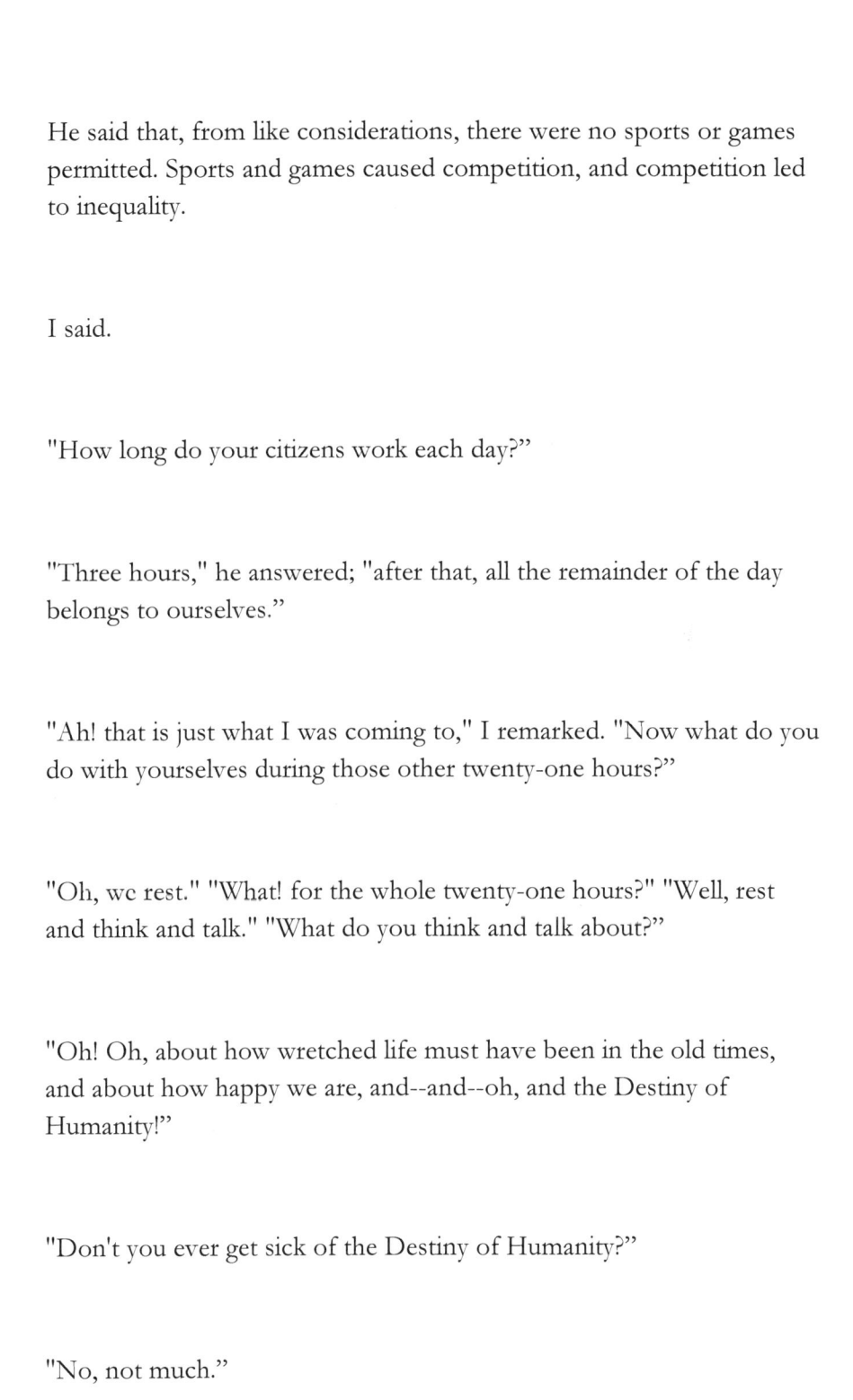

He said that, from like considerations, there were no sports or games permitted. Sports and games caused competition, and competition led to inequality.

I said.

"How long do your citizens work each day?"

"Three hours," he answered; "after that, all the remainder of the day belongs to ourselves."

"Ah! that is just what I was coming to," I remarked. "Now what do you do with yourselves during those other twenty-one hours?"

"Oh, we rest." "What! for the whole twenty-one hours?" "Well, rest and think and talk." "What do you think and talk about?"

"Oh! Oh, about how wretched life must have been in the old times, and about how happy we are, and--and--oh, and the Destiny of Humanity!"

"Don't you ever get sick of the Destiny of Humanity?"

"No, not much."

"And what do you understand by it? What is the Destiny of Humanity, do you think?"

"Oh!--why to--to go on being like we are now, only more so--everybody more equal, and more things done by electricity, and everybody to have two votes instead of one, and --"

"Thank you. That will do. Is there anything else that you think of? Have you got a religion?"

"Oh, yes."

"And you worship a God?"

"Oh, yes."

"What do you call him?"

"THE MAJORITY."

"One question more--You don't mind my asking you all these questions, by-the-by, do you?"

"Oh, no. This is all part of my three hours' labour for the State."

"Oh, I'm glad of that. I should not like to feel that I was encroaching on your time for rest; but what I wanted to ask was, do many of the people here commit suicide?"

"No; such a thing never occurs to them."

I looked at the faces of the men and women that were passing. There was a patient, almost pathetic, expression upon them all. I wondered where I had seen that look before; it seemed familiar to me.

All at once I remembered. It was just the quiet, troubled, wondering expression that I had always noticed upon the faces of the horses and oxen that we used to breed and keep in the old world.

* * *

Strange! how very dim and indistinct all the faces are around me! And where is my guide? and why am I sitting on the pavement? and--hark! surely that is the voice of Mrs. Biggles, my old landlady. Has she been asleep a thousand years, too? She says it is twelve o'clock--only twelve?

and I'm not to be washed 'til half-past four; and I do feel so stuffy and hot, and my head is aching. Hulloa! why, I'm in bed! Has it all been a dream.

And am I back in the nineteenth century.

Through the open window I hear the rush and roar of old life's battle. Men are fighting, striving, carving out each man his own life with the sword of strength and will. Men are laughing, grieving, loving, doing wrong deeds, doing great deeds,--falling, struggling, helping one another--living.

And I have a good deal more than three hours' work to do today, and I meant to be up at seven; and, oh dear! I do wish I had not smoked so many strong cigars last night.

THE END

Printed in Great Britain
by Amazon